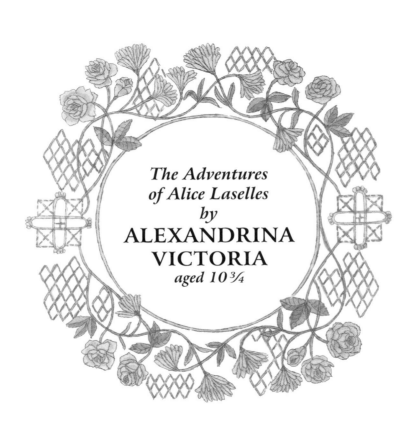

The Adventures
of Alice Laselles
by
ALEXANDRINA
VICTORIA
aged 10 ¾

The illustrations in this book were created by four very different people: firstly Queen Victoria and her governess Baroness Lehzen; and secondly Cristina Pieropan and Felix Petruška.

Once she had read the story very carefully, Cristina began designing the illustrations for it using a technique called 'etching'. This is a traditional process of making prints from a metal plate. In this process, the plate is first covered with wax and a special needle is used to scratch the drawing for the illustration onto the plate. The lines left by the needle will become the lines of the drawing. The plate is then covered in acid which carves the lines of the drawing into the metal, the rest of the wax is cleaned off, ink is pushed into the lines, and a sheet of paper is placed on the plate and run through a printing press. It's a very careful and painstaking process – and quite smelly and quite dangerous when the plate is sunk in its acid-bath!

Before she covered the zinc plates with wax, Cristina 'aged' the plates by scrubbing them with a metal brush. She did this because she wanted the illustrations to look as if they had been made a long, long time ago – as long ago as when Victoria first wrote her story. You can see some of the scratches made by the scrubbing in the final illustrations.

Queen Victoria's paper dolls were digitally cut out and manipulated by Felix Petruška, whose job it was to bring the paper dolls to life. He did this by changing their poses and expressions and by adding shadows to give them a more three-dimensional appearance.

The animated dolls were then set in their new home, Mrs Duncombe's school for girls, and the story was ready to begin.

*The Adventures
of Alice Laselles
by*
**ALEXANDRINA
VICTORIA**
aged 10¾

With an introduction by Jacqueline Wilson

ILLUSTRATIONS BY
CRISTINA PIEROPAN

Introduction

When I was a little girl I loved playing with paper dolls. My mother bought me paper doll cut-out books from toy shops, but these dolls were all too babyish to be inspiring. I preferred cutting out pictures of older girls and ladies in fashion pattern books. I'd give them all names and distinct personalities and play many elaborate imaginative games with them.

I didn't have any male figures so I couldn't divide my paper dolls up into families with fathers and brothers. My games were all set in boarding schools and orphanages for girls. Perhaps that's why I chose to write about Tracy Beaker when I grew up. My favourite of all my fictional heroines is Victorian Hetty Feather, who lives in a Foundling Hospital. I've always loved the Victorian age so it was a treat writing about her.

I was delighted and astonished to discover that the most famous of all Victorians, Queen Victoria herself, also loved paper dolls when she was a child. Her governess drew them for her, but the young Victoria coloured them in herself. I think you'll agree that she was very talented. Whenever I used my paintbox as a child I went over the lines and the colours bled into each other. I certainly couldn't manage sophisticated shading or attempt tiny patterns.

Victoria wasn't just very skilled with her brushwork. She was an eloquent and inventive writer too. She wrote this delightful story when she was ten. Alice's stepmother doesn't like her and persuades her father to send her to boarding school. There's no mention of holidays. Alice has to stay away for six whole years! This is a sad storyline after my own heart.

Victoria introduces us to each girl at the boarding school. They're a very interesting and varied bunch. I felt very sorry for little orphaned Ernestine and her unfortunate appearance, but my favourite of all the girls is naughty Diana whose violent temper makes her behave 'in a most indecorous manner'.

There's an interesting plot about a kitten and the tale ends happily, if a little hurriedly. Victoria was obviously keen to get to the end of her story. I know the feeling! If Victoria hadn't been destined to be Queen I think she might have made a remarkable novelist. I hope you enjoy her book.

Jacqueline Wilson

This book belongs to

....

To my dear Mamma
this
my first attempt at
composition
is affectionately and
dutifully inscribed
by her affectionate
daughter
Victoria.

O h do not send me away dear Pappa,' exclaimed Alice Laselles, as she threw her arms around her Pappa's neck; 'don't send me away, O let me stay with you.' And she sobbed bitterly.

'Dear Alice it is necessary for you to go my love, so go to bed my dear, and be ready for me tomorrow morning,' replied her father.

Poor Alice wept bitterly as she left the room and slowly crept upstairs. The above conversation proceeded from Colonel Laselles having told his little daughter, a lovely girl of twelve years old, that she must accompany him the next morning to Mrs Duncombe's school, a lady who lived about 30 miles from Laselles Hall, and who took in 8 young ladies at a time. She was highly recommended for her great respectability, amiability and sweetness of temper.

Colonel Laselles had the misfortune to lose his wife about 2 years ago by whom he had only one child, Alice. After she had been dead about a year he married a beautiful young lady only seventeen years old and by whom he now had a second daughter. But young Mrs Laselles did not like poor Alice. She always hinted to her husband that the girl would be much happier at school among other girls. At first Colonel Laselles would not hear of parting from his only child – his pretty, mild Alice - but when he became the father of a second little girl and Mrs Laselles told him he neglected both mother and daughter for Alice, he weakly consented to send her to school for six years, when she would be of an age to be able to go out in company.

Poor Alice got up with a heavy heart and swollen eyes the next day and prepared herself for her journey. The idea of not seeing her once happy home for six years was terrible to her. She could not think of parting from her dear Pappa and of not seeing her little sister Rose, whom she loved so to fondle, and her dog Frisk, and her black pony Bob.

At last Colonel Laselles called her to say goodbye to her unworthy and selfish stepmother. As she kissed her little sister's warm cheek the big tears rolled down her lovely face and she wept sadly.

'Come don't cry so, love,' said Mrs Laselles, 'think of all the pretty girls you'll see soon.'

But Alice was not so much of a child not to see that her departure was the work of her stepmother and she sullenly left the room and followed her Pappa downstairs where she took leave, with many tears, of poor Frisk.

'Pray take care of him,' said she to Martha the housekeeper, 'and don't forget to give him his bread and milk for breakfast and his toast and butter for supper.'

'You need not fear, miss,' said the good woman, 'for I dearly love Frisk myself for your sake.'

She then entered the chaise and cried almost the whole way. When they were about five miles from the school her father told her that she must dry her tears and cheer up as they would soon be there. At length the chaise stopped before a large house, which had the appearance of a cottage. The door had a porch which was overgrown with rose and honeysuckle, and ivy overhung the windows.

They were shown into a pretty little parlour by a servant who said that her mistress would come directly.

In about five minutes Mrs Duncombe appeared. She had a friendly open countenance, and was between forty and fifty, with firmly marked features. 'I fear Sir I have kept you waiting,' she said as she entered the room, 'but my young people were just going to dinner and I always dine with them, else I would have been ready to receive you Sir.'

'Pardon me madam,' replied Colonel Laselles, 'we have just arrived. Here is my daughter,' he added, taking Alice, who vainly strove to hide her tears, by the arm. 'She is just twelve years old.'

'I hope the young lady will soon become acquainted with her companions. Will you Sir partake of some refreshment with my young people?'

'Certainly madam. Take off your bonnet Alice and come with us.' Alice did as her father told her and taking his hand followed Mrs Duncombe into a large room where all the girls were at dinner, laughing and talking in high glee. At dinner Colonel Laselles explained to Mrs Duncombe all that he wished his daughter to learn and when the repast was finished he strained his daughter once more to his bosom and departed.

After her first effusion of grief was over Mrs Duncombe took Alice gently by the hand and said to her, 'Would you like me to show you up to your room?'

'Yes if you please madam,' replied the poor girl.

Mrs Duncombe then showed her upstairs to a nice little room overlooking the garden full of pretty flowers. Its furniture consisted of a small bed, a table, two chairs, a chest of drawers, a dressing table and book-shelf. Alice seemed much pleased with her lodgings and said, 'This is a sweet little room, and what a beautiful garden you have got.'

'I am glad that you like it my dear,' said Mrs D. 'Shall I send for your things?' Alice was about to answer when Betty the servant entered bringing her trunk. 'Oh here they come,' she said. 'I am busy my dear Alice therefore I must leave you for a short time but I will soon return to see if you want anything.' Mrs D then went away and left Alice occupied with Betty in unpacking her things.

In about a quarter of an hour she returned. 'What is this, my love?' said Mrs D, taking up a small red case.

'O,' said Alice, 'it is more valuable to me than all the diamonds and pearls of the world, it contains the greatest treasure I possess.' As she said this she pulled off the red case, and unlocked a little wooden box from which she took a string of hair to which was attached a locket with a lock of hair in it. 'It is my dear Mamma's dying gift. But if you should like to hear about it I will tell you.'

'I should like it very much my dear,' said Mrs D.

'About two months before my poor Mamma died she cut off a long piece of her beautiful black hair, and as she could plait very well she made it into this string and put a lock of her hair into this locket. Well, when she felt her last moment approaching she called me faintly to her bed, and taking this string and locket from her neck said, "This is my work, my hair – and my last gift. Always keep it by you and always remember your dying mother's last words."'

Mrs Duncombe was much touched by this recital and said, 'But have you no picture of this excellent mother?'

'Oh yes, I have,' said Alice, while she unclasped a small gold bracelet with her mother's picture which encircled her arm and holding it up said, 'There, look at this, this is my poor dear Mamma, and it is so like her too; Pappa gave it to me 3 years ago on my birth-day.'

At these words all the recollections of her home returned with full force and the poor girl began to cry so violently that Mrs D, fearing she might hurt herself, said, 'My dear girl I fear that so violent grief will only hurt you, so when you feel a little more composed you may come downstairs and see the girls dance.'

Mrs D then left her to compose herself until 4 o'clock when she reappeared and told her that the dancing would then begin. Alice felt better now and though very sad still she gladly accepted her kind Mistress's invitation.

Before we go on it would be as well perhaps to
introduce our readers to the young people of
Mrs D's establishment.

Barbara Somerville,
who had been longest in the school,
and consequently claims our attention first,
was the daughter of a rich banker in London,
but his wife being passionately fond
of the world he felt compelled to send Barbara
to school at the age of 10, where she had now
been 6 years and was about to return home.
She was a tall slender girl of a dark
complexion with fine regular features
but an unconquerable pride, which in spite
of all Mrs D's efforts to subdue it still remained,
spoiled her otherwise fine expression.
She was a very clever girl and learned
every thing better than any
other girl in the school.

The next who claims our attention
was a poor little French orphan
called Ernestine Duval, whose parents
having died when she was quite young,
she was left to the charge of an uncle,
who being rather poor and having many
children of his own to provide for,
sent her to Mrs D's school, in preference
to one in her own country.
He was her maternal uncle and therefore
English, his sister having married M. Duval
in Paris when her father was there on business.
Poor Ernestine had now been 3 years
with Mrs D and was the most gentle
and affectionate child but her personal
deformities rendered her unprepossessing
to her more fortunate companions.
She was very short and broad,
her face dreadfully scarred and pocked
by the small pox, by which malady
she had lost one eye.

Charlotte Graves who came next
was a perfect model of beauty.
She was the only child of a widow who having
married a man much younger than herself
when her daughter was already 14 years old
sent her to school, where she was
to remain until she was 19.
She was at this period just seventeen
and there never was seen a more lovely little
creature than she was. She was not tall
but had a nice little figure, she had dark brown
eyes, a small nose, a very pretty mouth
with beautiful teeth and light brown hair which
she wore in ringlets in front
and twisted round her head at the back.
Her complexion was not fair but very clear with
rosy cheeks. Having thus painted
as well as I could the appearance of this young
beauty it will be necessary to say a little about
her character. Vanity and affectation
were her predominate qualities, accompanied
by a great mildness or rather more lazy
quietness. She paid proper attention
to her lessons but all her leisure time
was employed in arranging her curls
with the greatest care under a small straw
bonnet when she went out or with combs
on each side when at home.

Laura and Adelaide Burtin
were twins and had arrived but 4 months.
They had been sent by their parents who were
gone to India, to remain only for a year.
They were unoffending
good sort of girls.

Diana O'Reilly had been a year at the school.
She was the most extraordinary girl.
Her father, Capt O'Reilly, had married a very
young and beautiful Irish lady who died at
Diana's birth. He was so distracted at her death
that leaving his only child with a nurse he set
sail for India where he remained 10 years.
When he returned he found Di,
as she was generally called, in a state of perfect
ignorance. As he entered the cottage of the
nurse he asked where his child was,
upon which the woman pointed to a tall girl of
a most uncouth appearance.
A quantity of black disheveled hair was
streaming over her back and face; her dress
consisted of a coarse shift, which hung loosely
about her, and displayed two brawny red arms,
and a coarse jagged blue petticoat with bare
legs and feet. She was kneeling on the ground
scolding the little boys and girls. Capt O'Reilly
hid his face in his hands and was horrified.
He advanced toward her saying that he was
her father upon which she answered him in a
brogue so unintelligible that he almost started.
He directly took her away and sent her to school
for 8 years. For the first two months poor Di
was the most miserable being possible; the
shoes and stockings she was obliged to wear
pinched and hurt her sadly, and every restraint
made her scream. She had temper beyond
anything, so violent even Mrs D's mildness
could not subdue it.

The last girl in the school was Selina Bawden,
a most delightful sweet-tempered creature but
unfortunately she was both deaf and dumb.
Both her parents were dead and her rich
unmarried uncle who disliked children sent her
to school at the age of 8 where she had
now been two years.

Alice's first introduction was awkward. The girls stared at her and she felt so shy that she did not like to approach them. Mrs D perceiving their mutual embarrassment said, 'Come Barbara you ought to make acquaintance with your new companion. Charlotte, Di, Selina, come loves and don't look so shy.'

Barbara with some difficulty overcame her pride and going up to little Alice said in a protecting tone of voice, 'Pray how old are you?'

Alice bashfully answered, '12 years old, Miss.' She then took courage and struck by Selina's mild gentle expression went up to her and said, 'How long have you been here?'

Selina shook her head and looked very sad. Alice repeated her question and Selina then pointing to her lips and ears again shook her head.

'Pray mam, what is the matter with this girl?' asked Alice of Mrs D.

'She is both deaf and dumb my love,' was the answer. 'But Charlotte or Barbara can show you in a very few minutes how to speak to her by means of your fingers.'

'I will show you how!' exclaimed Ernestine and she instantly began talking to her upon her fingers and Selina smiled and nodded. She went up to Alice and kissed her. Alice then seated herself beside Ernestine while the others danced and she showed her how to talk.

Selina came toward Alice and smiling pointed toward her companions who were dancing as if to say, 'Will you not join them?' But poor Alice was not in a dancing mood, sadness still hung over her and the thought of home made the tears trickle down her cheeks.

After dancing was over the girls repaired to their own rooms to study till 7 then dinner hour. Mrs D called Alice to her and said, 'Have you now made acquaintance with your companions?'

'O yes Mam, Selina and Ernestine are quite delightful.'

'I am glad my dear that you have found friendship with two such nice girls as Selina and Ernestine. The former is a pattern of mildness and resignation, to a fate which is indeed a very hard one, and would be far more so were her misfortune not so wonderfully compensated by her extreme quickness of perception and cheerful disposition. Ernestine is likewise a dear creature. Her situation in point of life and appearance is far more unfortunate than Selina's as her face is so very plain and her being a stranger in a land quite unknown to her until she came here.'

As Mrs D concluded Barbara ran up to her and whispered something into her ear at which Mrs D seemed much displeased and gave her a look of stern displeasure. 'No Barbara that cannot be I am sure, Miss Laselles would not venture to do such a thing without asking me.'

'What Mam,' exclaimed Alice 'what about me?'

'Why I have just heard from Barbara Somerville that you have placed a cat in my kitchen without previously enquiring from me if such a thing was allowed. Now I never permit any cat whatsoever to be in the kitchen or the house and particularly not without permission. I shall therefore beg of you my dear Alice to send your cat home to Laselles Hall.'

'Indeed Mam I never even had a cat for Pappa does not like them, and as for venturing to bring a cat into your house, I never dreamt of doing so undutiful a thing, indeed Mam it is not my cat.'

'Well then Miss Benson our teacher must tell a lie for it was she who told me that she saw the cat with a piece of red ribbon round its neck on which was written Alice Laselles,' retorted Barbara.

'No no I never brought one, somebody must have done so out of malice, out of pure unkindness, to a poor helpless stranger,' sobbed out poor Alice.

'Come, come my good girl I dare say there is some mistake about it. Go up to your room my dear and I shall try to make out this confusion.'

Alice went upstairs crying and would have gone on so had she not thought and reasoned with herself, and as she knew she was innocent what reason had she to fret and cry? The truth always comes out sooner or later.

So it proved with Alice. Accordingly when she heard the supper bell she combed her hair and making herself look tidy and neat she slowly walked down the passage when she heard sobs and screams and in a very few minutes beheld Miss Benson leading Di upstairs, who was struggling and screaming in a most indecorous manner as she always did when she was in a passion, which occurred alas almost every other day. The cause was soon explained for Alice met Ernestine halfway upstairs whose whole countenance beamed with joy. 'Dear Alice,' said she, 'Mrs D has found out the whole, the mystery is disclosed and your innocence is proved. Trivial as the occurrence about the cat appeared, our dear good governess always makes a point to find out the truth, so accordingly we were all assembled, Miss Benson and Nanny the cook also. Di alone was not forthcoming and can you believe it, O Alice she was the culprit.'

'Really,' said Alice.

'Yes she was. The story is this which Nanny told us and which Di in a great rage was forced to confess. Mrs Martin the farmer's wife made Di the present of a beautiful kitten which Di managed to hide in her bed-room for a whole month; when the kitten was getting too large she bribed Nanny by fine words to conceal her in the kitchen which she did. When you arrived she mischievously thought out of frolic she would put your name on Puss's collar, which she did and Miss Benson seeing it told it to Barbara. Now dear Alice come down and receive a kiss from our dear governess and from us all except Di who is in penitence until tomorrow morning.'

Alice as we may suppose was much pleased, though she knew before she was innocent. She was received with open arms by Mrs D and all the girls except Barbara who protected Di. As soon as supper was over the girls seated themselves around a large oaken table while Mrs D read aloud some historical book for an hour and they worked. After that they amused themselves till bed-time.

Alice the next morning rose with a light heart and attended to her lessons so well that in less than 3 months she was one of the best learners in the school.

THE END

The Story of the Story of The Adventures of Alice Laselles

We think Queen Victoria wrote this story when she was just coming up to her eleventh birthday. As you can see, she wrote it as a schoolroom exercise in English 'Composition', and dedicated it to 'her dear Mamma'. It's a pretty long story to have been written by someone who was only 10¾, but Victoria loved writing – she kept a journal, or diary, from the age of 13, and wrote in it every day. You can see that even when she was a child, she was someone who loved words.

She also had a very good imagination. Lots of children make up friends who are invisible to everyone else, but Victoria made up a whole school full of them, and a family at home for little Alice as well. Her story, in its red notebook, is now kept in the Royal Archives at Windsor Castle. In fact, the whole thing is a little bit longer than the adventure printed here. We thought the story of Alice, and her arrival at school, and then the mystery of who put the cat in Mrs Duncombe's kitchen, made a complete tale on its own. So we decided to end this book at the point where Alice is happily settled into school and in fact has become one of its 'best learners'.

Then of course the story had to have illustrations. Victoria and her governess made many, many dolls, some of which were on paper. We think Baroness Lehzen, her governess, drew them and helped Victoria colour them in, but some may have been coloured in by Victoria herself – she was good at art, too. There are two albums of these paper dolls, also kept safely in the Royal Archives. They are illustrated on the next two pages, so you can see what the dolls we have used as characters in this story look like in real life. She and Baroness Lehzen would also tell each other stories as Victoria had her hair brushed.

Victoria was born on 24 May 1819. Her father, the Duke of Kent, died when she was only eight months old, and she was brought up by her mother at Kensington Palace. Although she was known as 'Drina' when she was little, from the age of about her 5, she used her 2nd name, Victoria. As a grown-up, she described her childhood as 'rather melancholy', meaning lonely and sad – she was allowed to mix with very few children of her own age, but she did have a half-sister, Princess Feodora. The two princesses were very fond of each other, but when Victoria was 9 Feodora, who was 12 years older than her, married a German prince and went to live in Germany. So just like Alice, Victoria knew how sad it could make you, to be separated from people you loved. Victoria also had pets – a grey pony and a dog too.

Victoria did not realise she was to be Queen one day until she was 11 years old. She became queen when she was just 18, in 1837, and in 1840 married her cousin, Prince Albert – and so the Victorian age began.

Alexandrina Victoria's Paper Dolls

We think Queen Victoria made these paper dolls in about 1830 –
about the same time as she wrote down the story of Alice's adventures,
and about the same year as she was painted by the artist Richard Westall.
You can see his portrait of Victoria on page 4 of this book.

Some of the dolls were probably painted by Victoria's half-sister, Princess Feodora, and some by the daughter of Sir John Conroy, who was in charge of the household at Kensington Palace, where Victoria grew up. They were carefully cut out and pasted into two books, which are now kept safe in the Royal Archives. The dolls all seem to have had names – so perhaps Victoria and her governess, Baroness Lehzen, made up stories about them.

If you would like to find out more about the books and paintings
and all the other items in the Royal Collection, as well as about the royal palaces
and the Royal Family, you can do so by visiting our website
www.royalcollection.org.uk

Published 2015 by Royal Collection Trust
York House
St James's Palace
London SW1A 1BQ

Find out more about the Royal Collection and Palaces at www.royalcollection.org.uk
Subscribe to Royal Collection Trust's e-Newsletter at www.royalcollection.org.uk/newsletter

Royal Collection Trust / © HM Queen Elizabeth II 2015
Introduction © Jacqueline Wilson 2015

ISBN 978 1 909741 18 8

015260

British Library Cataloguing in Publication data:
A catalogue record of this book is available from the British Library.

Project Manager and Editor: Debbie Bibo
Book and Cover Designer: Duška Karanov
Doll Animations by Felix Petruška

Typeset in Acta and Arrus
Printed on Munken Pure Rough
Colour reproduction by UnoUndici, Verona
Printed and bound in Turkey by Ofset Yapimevi

All works reproduced are Royal Collection Trust / © HM Queen Elizabeth II 2015

Page 4:
Richard Westall (1765-1836), *Queen Victoria* (1819-1901) *when a girl*, 1830 (detail).
Oil on canvas, 145.8 x 115 cm, RCIN 400135